Grandpa and Thomas
and the Green Umbrella

PUFFIN BOOKS

Published by the Penguin Group
Penguin Group (Australia)
250 Camberwell Road, Camberwell, Victoria 3124, Australia
(a division of Pearson Australia Group Pty Ltd)
Penguin Group (USA) Inc.
375 Hudson Street, New York, New York 10014, USA
Penguin Group (Canada)
90 Eglinton Avenue East, Suite 700,
Toronto ON M4P 2Y3, Canada
(a division of Pearson Penguin Canada Inc.)
Penguin Books Ltd
80 Strand, London WC2R 0RL, England
Penguin Ireland
25 St Stephen's Green, Dublin 2, Ireland
(a division of Penguin Books Ltd)
Penguin Books India Pvt Ltd
11 Community Centre, Panchsheel Park, New Delhi – 110 017, India
Penguin Group (NZ)
67 Apollo Drive, Rosedale, North Shore 0632, New Zealand
(a division of Pearson New Zealand Ltd)
Penguin Books (South Africa) (Pty) Ltd
24 Sturdee Avenue, Rosebank, Johannesburg 2196, South Africa

Penguin Books Ltd, Registered Offices: 80 Strand, London, WC2R 0RL, England
First published by Penguin Group (Australia), a division of Pearson Australia Group Pty Ltd, 2006

This paperback edition published by Penguin Group (Australia), 2009

10 9 8 7 6 5 4 3 2 1

Designed by Deborah Brash © Penguin Group (Australia)
Typeset in 24/30pt Minister Light by Deborah Brash
Separations by Splitting Image Colour Studio, Victoria
Printed and bound by Everbest Printing, China

National Library of Australia
Cataloguing-in-Publication data:

Allen, Pamela.
Grandpa and Thomas and the green umbrella

ISBN 978 0 14 350368 2

1. Grandfathers - Juvenile fiction. 2. Grandparent and child -
Juvenile fiction. I. Title.

A823.3

puffin.com.au

Grandpa and Thomas

and the Green Umbrella

Pamela Allen

Puffin Books

For Thomas and Toby

Grandpa and Thomas go to the beach.
The gulls are screeching and the sea is singing.

The sun is hot.
Grandpa and Thomas spread out the big
picnic rug and put up the green umbrella.
Thomas wears his hat.
Grandpa does too.
'You'll need sunscreen,' says Grandpa.
'You'll need some too,' says Thomas.

Grandpa builds a car.
Thomas does too.
'Brm! Brm! Brm!' goes Thomas.

Grandpa goes in the water.
Thomas does too.
'Look, Grandpa,' cries Thomas. 'I can swim.'

Grandpa draws in the sand.
Thomas does too.

'See, *Thomas*,'

says Grandpa.

Grandpa throws a stick way out to sea.
Thomas does too.
'All gone,' says Thomas.

Thomas slides down the sand hill.
Grandpa does too.
'OOOOOOH,' cries Grandpa.

'Hungry?' asks Grandpa.
'Mmm-mm,' says Thomas.
'I am too,' says Grandpa.

The sun is going.
Grandpa shivers.
'I'm getting dressed,' says Grandpa.
'I am too,' says Thomas.

Now the sun has gone and the wind is blowing.
Suddenly the green umbrella flies bowling and
bobbing away.
'Catch it,' cries Thomas.
Grandpa runs fast.
Thomas does too.

'Got it,' gasps Grandpa.
Grandpa is puffing and panting.
Thomas is too.
'Hurry, it's going to rain,' cries Grandpa.

Then the rain comes.

'Time to go,' bellows Grandpa, grabbing up their things.
'Quick,' says Thomas. 'Get in the car.'
Thomas climbs in.
Grandpa does too.

It is cold. The sky is black, the wind is blowing, the gulls are screeching and the rain is falling.

'I'll drive,' says Thomas.
'Brm! Brm! Brm! Brm! Brm! Brm!'
and he does.
'Brm! Brm! Brm! Brm! Brm! Brm!'

until the rain stops
and the wind drops.
Thomas climbs out of the car.
Grandpa does too.
Thomas folds up the big picnic rug.
Grandpa takes down the green umbrella.

'I'm warm and dry,' says Thomas.
'I am too,' says Grandpa.